Shoo! Scat!

by

Lois G. Grambling

illustrated by

Barbara Johansen Newman

Marshall Cavendish

New York • London • Singapore

To my husband, and only he knows why;
of course, now Margery and Judy, know too.
—L. G. G.

For my son Ben, my studio mate and
an aspiring artist in his own right.
—B.J.N.

Marshall Cavendish
99 White Plains Road
Tarrytown, NY 10591
www.marshallcavendish.com

Library of Congress Cataloging-in-Publication Data

Grambling, Lois G.
Shoo! scat! / by Lois G. Grambling ; illustrated by Barbara Johansen Newman.– 1st ed.
p. cm.
Summary: Professor Flugel builds a bird feeder, but instead of enjoying the birds,
he finds himself trying to outwit Gray Squirrel, who keeps scaring the birds away, until
he figures out a way to be friends.
ISBN 0-7614-5167-6
[1. Problem solving—Fiction. 2. Squirrels—Fiction. 3. Friendship—Fiction.]
I. Newman, Barbara Johansen, ill. II. Title.

PZ7.G7655Sho 2004
[E]—dc22
2004000867

The text of this book is set in Comic Strip Classic.
The illustrations are rendered in acrylic gouache on watercolor paper.
Book design by Adam Mietlowski

Printed in China

First edition

1 3 5 6 4 2

PROFESSOR Flugel was building a splendid new bird feeder.

When it was finished, he put it on
a wooden post in his backyard.

At breakfast the next morning, Professor Flugel sat and enjoyed the many birds that came to feed. And he was happy. But not for long, because . . .

quick as a flash, Gray Squirrel climbed up the wooden post, thumped onto the porch (frightening away all the birds), and started eating.

Professor Flugel was furious! He banged on his kitchen window. "Shoo! Scat!" he shouted. "Go away!"

But Gray Squirrel did not go away. Instead he waved at the professor and continued eating.

Professor Flugel banged on his kitchen window. Again. But Gray Squirrel did not pay any attention. He was too busy making a sign.

Please refill.
Sunflower seeds
would be nice.
See you tomorrow
for breakfast.
Have a good day.

Professor Flugel was not having a good day. All he could think about was Gray Squirrel eating the birdseed tomorrow. Understandably, Professor Flugel was upset.

Suddenly he had what he thought was a brilliant idea. . . .

The next morning, Professor Flugel got up early and refilled his splendid new bird feeder.

Then, holding his grandson's super-duper super-soaker, he hid behind a bush in his backyard.

Gray Squirrel had gotten up early, too, and had watched the professor.

Minutes later, wearing a raincoat, a rain hat, boots, and carrying a big umbrella, Gray Squirrel climbed up the wooden post, thumped onto the porch (frightening away all the birds), and started eating.

Professor Flugel was furious!

"Shoo! Scat!" he shouted. "*Go away!*" He squirted his grandson's super-duper super-soaker.

But Gray Squirrel did not go away. Instead he opened his big umbrella and continued to eat.

In minutes Professor Flugel's splendid new bird feeder was empty. *Again.* So Gray Squirrel made another sign.

Please refill.
Sunflower seeds and thistle would be nice.
See you tomorrow for breakfast.
Have a good day.

Professor Flugel was not having a good day. All he could think about was Gray Squirrel eating the birdseed tomorrow. Understandably, Professor Flugel was very upset.

Suddenly he had what he thought was a brilliant idea. . . .

The next morning, Professor Flugel got up early and refilled his splendid new bird feeder. Then he rented a backhoe, dug a deep moat, and filled it with water and one lean alligator.

But Gray Squirrel had gotten up early, too, and had watched the professor.

Minutes later, wearing
a wet suit and snorkeling gear
and carrying a bait bag filled
with raw meat, Gray Squirrel
tossed the raw meat to the
lean alligator, snorkeled over
to the splendid new bird feeder, thumped onto
the porch (frightening away all the birds), and
started eating.

In minutes Professor Flugel's splendid new bird feeder was empty. *Again.* So Gray Squirrel made another sign.

Please refill. Sunflower seeds, thistle and cracked corn would be nice. See you tomorrow for breakfast.
Have a good day.

Professor Flugel was not having a good day. All he could think about was Gray Squirrel eating the birdseed tomorrow. Understandably, Professor Flugel was very, VERY upset!

Suddenly he had what he thought was a brilliant idea. . . .

The next morning, Professor Flugel got up early, filled in the deep moat, returned the alligator to the pet store, and refilled his bird feeder.

He took down the wooden post and replaced it with a tall, smooth metal pole that not even a sharp-clawed Gray Squirrel could climb. Then, he moved everything in his kitchen to his roof.

But Gray Squirrel had gotten up early, too, and had watched the professor.

Minutes later, wearing an aviator's helmet and big goggles, a leather jacket and a jaunty scarf, Gray Squirrel drifted over to the splendid new bird feeder in a hot air balloon. He thumped down on the porch (frightening away all the birds), and started eating.

FLAKES

In minutes Professor Flugel's splendid new bird feeder was empty. *Again.* So Gray Squirrel made another sign.

Then he climbed back into the hot air balloon and drifted away.

Professor Flugel was not having a good day. All he could think about was Gray Squirrel eating the birdseed tomorrow. He was very, very, VERY upset!

Suddenly he had an idea. It was not a brilliant idea, but it was the only idea Professor Flugel had.

The next morning, Professor Flugel got up early and made a sign.

He put the sign in his kitchen window, hurried up to the roof, and moved everything from his kitchen back down to where it belonged. Then, he replaced the tall, smooth metal pole with the wooden post and refilled his feeder.

Minutes later, wearing his bathrobe and slippers, Gray Squirrel knocked on Professor Flugel's door. He was carrying a sign.

From that morning on, Professor Flugel and Gray Squirrel sat together at the kitchen table, eating toast and sunflower seeds, drinking tea, and enjoying the birds.

Professor Flugel was happy. But not for long. Because . . .

high in a tall oak
tree a young squirrel
was watching . . .